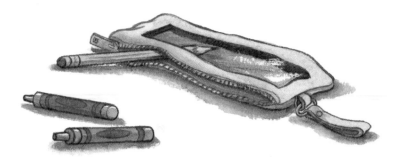

MY FIRST
I Can Read Book®

Biscuit Goes to School

story by ALYSSA SATIN CAPUCILLI
pictures by PAT SCHORIES

HarperCollins*Publishers*

HarperCollins®, 🦃®, and I Can Read Book®
are trademarks of HarperCollins Publishers Inc.

Biscuit Goes to School
Text copyright © 2002 by Alyssa Satin Capucilli
Illustrations copyright © 2002 by Pat Schories
Printed in the U.S.A. All rights reserved.
www.harperchildrens.com

Library of Congress Cataloging-in-Publication Data
Capucilli, Alyssa.
 Biscuit goes to school / story by Alyssa Satin Capucilli ; pictures by Pat Schories.
  p.   cm.
 Summary: A dog follows the bus to school, where he meets the teacher and takes part
in the activities of the class.
 ISBN 0-06-028682-2 — ISBN 0-06-028683-0 (lib. bdg.)
 ISBN 0–06–443616-0 (pbk.)
 [1. Dogs—Fiction.   2. Schools—Fiction.]   I. Schories, Pat, ill.   II. Title.
III. Series.
PZ7.C179 Bisf   2002   00-049881
[E]—dc21

❖

For the wonderful students, teachers, librarians, and parents who have welcomed Biscuit into their schools!

Here comes the school bus!

Woof, woof!

Stay here, Biscuit.

Dogs don't go to school.

Woof!

Where is Biscuit going?

Is Biscuit going to the pond?

Woof!

Is Biscuit going to the park?
Woof!

Biscuit is going to school!
Woof, woof!

Biscuit wants to play ball.

Woof, woof!

Biscuit wants
to hear a story.
Woof, woof!
Shhh!

Biscuit wants a snack.

Woof, woof!

Oh, Biscuit!

What are you doing here?

Dogs don't go to school!

17

Oh, no!

Here comes the teacher!

Woof!

Biscuit wants
to meet the teacher.
Woof!

Biscuit wants
to meet the class.
Woof, woof!

Biscuit likes school!

Woof, woof!

And everyone at school
likes Biscuit!
Woof!

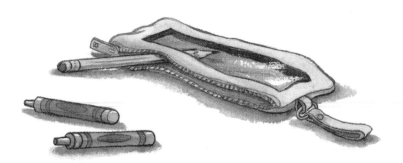